SILVER MOON

Fitzhenry & Whiteside Limited
195 Allstate Parkway
Markham, Ontario   L3R 4T8

In the United States:
121 Harvard Avenue, Suite 2
Allston, Massachusetts 02134

www.fitzhenry.ca   godwit@fitzhenry.ca

Fitzhenry & Whiteside acknowledges with thanks the Canada Council for the Arts, the Government of Canada through its Book Publishing Industry Development Program, and the Ontario Arts Council for their support of our publishing program.

National Library of Canada Cataloguing in Publication

Krykorka, Ian
Silver moon : Rusalka and other stories from Antonin Dvorak / by Ian Krykorka ;
illustrations by Vladyana Krykorka ; foreword by Josef Skvorecky.

ISBN 1-55041-684-7

1. Tales—Czech Republic. I. Dvorak, Antonin, 1841-1904 II. Krykorka, Vladyana III. Title.

PS8571.R94S54 2003   398.2'094371   C2003-902336-2
PR9199.4.K79S54 2003

U.S. Publisher Cataloging-in-Publication Data
(Library of Congress Standards)

Krykorka, Ian.
Silver moon : Rusalka and other stories from Antonin Dvorak / Ian Krykorka ; Vladyana
Krykorka. —1st ed.
[72] p. : ill. (chiefly col.) ; cm.
Summary: Enchantment was as thick as the trees, and young men and women
of all kinds met and fell in love under the spell of the silver moon. Czech composer,
Antonin Dvorak set some of the folk tales to music.
ISBN 1-55041-684-7
1. Tales, Czech. 2. Short stories, Czech. 3. Love stories, Czech. I. Dvorak, Antonin, 1841-1904. II.
Krykorka, Vladyana. III. Title.
891.8/ 6352 21   PG5038.K7956Si 2003

Design by Wycliffe Smith Design Inc.
Printed in Hong Kong

SILVER MOON

Stories from Antonin Dvorak's
most Enchanting Operas

IAN AND VLADYANA
KRYKORKA

FITZHENRY & WHITESIDE

*In memory
of my grandparents
Vladimir & Anna.*
I.K.

*To all opera lovers,
especially my husband
Jack Johnson*
V.K.

Antonin

ANTONIN DVORAK 1841–1904

From a butcher's boy, Antonin Dvorak grew into one of the great composers of the 19th century. He was mostly self-taught, with roots deeply embedded in Czech folksong, but he also absorbed the lessons of his great predecessors and contemporaries, his compatriot Bedrich Smetana *(The Bartered Bride)*, and the German master Johannes Brahms.

A brief but influential part of his life was his American sojourn (1891–1895) as Director of the National Conservatory of Music in New York. He was probably the first major composer to recognize the musical genius of Afro-American people whose songs he compared to the "best melodies of Beethoven". In works written in the United States he was clearly influenced by what he heard in America. Symphony No. 9. *From the New World*, with echoes of Negro spirituals and with the haunting English horn solo in the Largo, is a testimony to that side of Dvorak. But even the Cello Concerto in B Minor, composed shortly after his return to Bohemia—probably the most popular cello concerto in literature—resonates with his then-fresh memories of the sounds and

1841 · Antonin Dvořák · 1904

moods of the new continent. String Quartet in F Major, rich in pentatonic motifs, was written during his first American vacation in Spillville, Iowa and is justly known as "American". Unjustly neglected is another tribute to America, the beautiful Suite in A Major which likewise became known as "American".

Dvorak's views on the linking of transformed folklore with highbrow music was quite an innovative force among his students and his students' students, such as Aaron Copland, and with such composers as George Gershwin. Ninth Symphony's Largo reverberates in Duke Ellington ("Come Sunday" from the *Black, Brown and Beige Suite*) and its melody turned into a veritable folksong known as "Going Home" — not always known as Dvorak's composition. Another piece to become an often anonymous hit melody is Humoresque in G-flat Major, of which there exist numerous characteristically American renditions, including jazz arrangements by John Kirby and brilliant improvisations by performers such as the violinist Emilio Caceres or the Canadian virtuoso Oscar Peterson.

Dvorak

In this sense Dvorak is an integral part of American musical consciousness. Until recently however, his lovely operas were little known here. *Rusalka* (1901), the best known product of his last years, was in a way also conceived in America, for the incipient melody of its "Aria to the Moon" can be found in Dvorak's American music notebooks. But, of course, it's a thoroughly Czech work, saturated with folk fairy tales and legends and composed from the delicate lyrical libretto of the poet Jaroslav Kvapil.

The second opera in this selection, *The King and the Charcoal Burner* (1871), is Dvorak's first — a work of his formative years. It's based on the ancient migrating motif of a king learning the lessons of his simple subjects when, by accident, he moves among them unrecognized.

In contrast, *Kate and the Devil* (1888), is a delightful comic opera, also with echoes of Czech fairy tales, in which a courageous village girl voluntarily accompanies (and bullies) an unfortunate devil to hell and back. She springs not only from ancient village humor; she can also be seen as a curious prefiguration of the modern woman who, in a world of men and devils, has her own way.

Of Dvorak's many other works, perhaps the best or the best known are a magnificient orchestral piece "Scherzo Capriccioso," the popular two series of Slavonic Dances, nine symphonies, several string quartets and other chamber music compositions and the Violin Concerto in A Minor. He was a prolific music maker. And he was also a deeply religious man, as testifies his profound compositions, the cantata *Stabat Mater,* the moving *Te Deum,* and above all the exquisite *Biblical Songs* with lyrics taken from King David's psalms.

Antonin Dvorak is a national treasure to the Czechs and a student and teacher of much of what's best in American music.

Josef Skvorecky
Author of *Dvorak in Love,* a novel

RUSALKA

Lyrical fairy-tale opera

Libretto by Jaroslav Kvapil

First performed: National Theatre, Prague, March 31, 1901

THE KING AND THE CHARCOAL BURNER

Comic opera based on a fairy tale

Libretto by Bernard Guldener and Vaclav Juda Novotny

First performed: Czech Provisional Theatre, Prague, November 24, 1874.

KATE AND THE DEVIL

Opera based on a folk comedy

Libretto by Adolf Wenig

First performed: National Theatre, Prague, November 23, 1899

RUSALKA

Once upon a time, in an enchanting pool deep in the forests of Bohemia, there lived a water nymph. Her name was Rusalka and her beauty was legendary: her skin was as white as waterlily petals, her hair as fair as moonlight, her eyes the color of a clear summer sky reflected on the surface of a still pond. Most beautiful of all, though, was her shimmering voice. When Rusalka sang, all the creatures stopped what they were doing to listen, and even the wind was calmed.

One day, a prince and his hunting party, on their way home from a successful chase, happened to wander by the forest pool and hear Rusalka singing.

"You have the most beautiful voice I have ever heard," said the prince as he walked toward her. "Truly, I have never seen anyone like you in the whole world." He knelt down before her, and took her hand. "Please come back to my castle and be my guest of honor at dinner tonight."

Rusalka had never seen a human. The instant the prince touched her, she felt something stir deep within her.

"Man," she said, "come back when the moon is full." And with those words, she dove into the icy depths of the lake.

Rusalka

That night Rusalka swam to the far side of the lake to visit Jezibaba, the forest witch.

"Hello Rusalka, I have been expecting you," said Jezibaba, "and I know what you are about to ask me. I can grant your wish, but should you accept my help you will become as silent as the grave. And be warned: humans are not to be trusted."

Rusalka didn't heed this warning, and did not stop to contemplate the terrible price she would have to pay. "Oh, Jezibaba, I wish to taste human love and know human feelings. Help me become mortal so that I might experience these things," she exclaimed.

The witch then gave Rusalka a cup full of magic brew. The instant the water nymph drank it, her tail was transformed into legs and she became human.

When the moon was full, the prince returned to the lake where Rusalka was waiting for him. He embraced her.

"I have been thinking about you night and day ever since I last saw you and I want to be with you now more than ever. Come back to my castle and be my wife," he pleaded.

Rusalka smiled and nodded in reply.

"What is the matter? Can't you speak?"

Rusalka shook her head. She couldn't explain without her voice.

The prince was confused, but he was happy just to be with her.

He took her to his castle, and everyone thought the silent maiden was the kindest and gentlest person they had ever met. Her beautiful smile seemed to say more than a thousand words.

The prince and his family decided to have a celebration in Rusalka's honor. They invited hundreds of guests. Among them was a beautiful foreign princess, with raven-black hair and fire in her eyes. Strangely, no one seemed to know her.

The foreign princess had a divine voice, as powerful as Rusalka's had been, and throughout the night she used it, seducing the prince with songs. Rusalka tried to win back the prince's attention but he was so entranced with the mysterious woman's singing that it was as if Rusalka had never existed.

Rusalka was terribly wounded. She ran from the castle in tears, back to her forest home. When Rusalka arrived, Jezibaba appeared to her out of thin air. "I warned you about humans," she said coldly. "Did you see how easily I wooed him away from you? He didn't even recognize that it was your voice coming from the lips he gazed at so hungrily. Now your voice is gone, and you are changed forever. I can turn you back into a water nymph, but you will never forget the pain of losing your beloved."

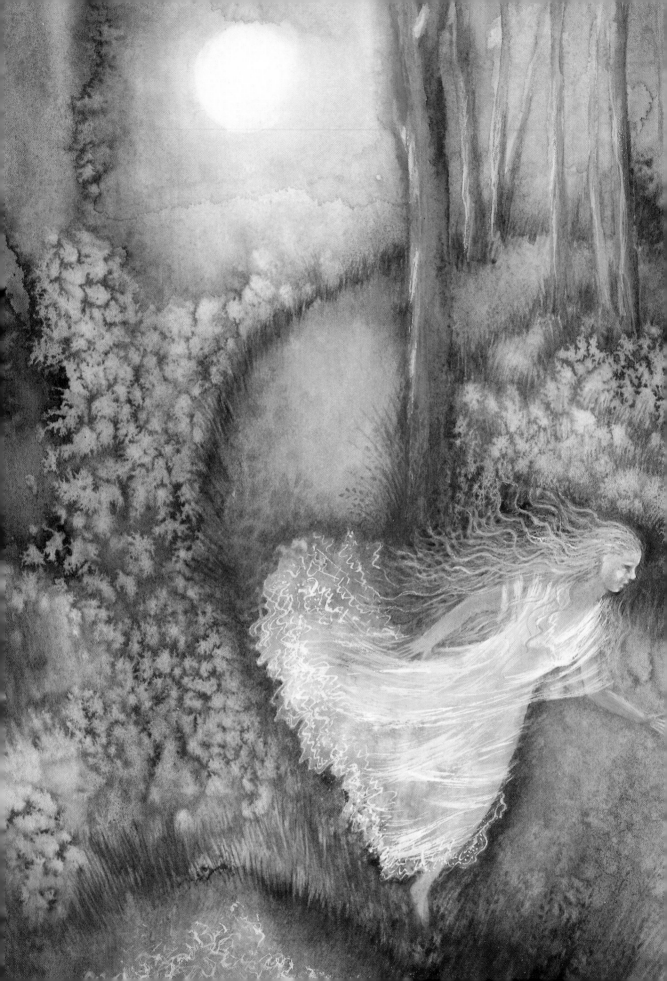

Meanwhile, the prince was searching everywhere in the castle and on the grounds for Rusalka. The witch's spell over him had broken as soon as she vanished. "How could I have hurt Rusalka so?" he lamented, cursing himself for being such a fool.

The prince's courtiers all missed Rusalka's kindness and beauty. And they were anxious about their prince, who was sick with grief and inconsolable.

"We will find Rusalka and convince her
to come back," vowed the prince's gamekeeper. He organized a search party and
went into the forest to look for Rusalka's
pool. When they found it, however, they
were frightened away by the witch, who knew
they had come for Rusalka. The gamekeeper
and his men returned to the castle empty-
handed.

But their efforts were not completely fruitless. Upon hearing of the gamekeeper's failure, the prince roused from his grief and set out on his own to find his lost love. He wandered through the forest, heartsick and weary, until at last he found Rusalka's home. Across the water he cried, "Oh, Rusalka, I cannot live without you! Please forgive me!"

From under the waves Rusalka heard his anguish and instantly forgave him. She rose to the surface and took his hand.

"I cannot live without you," the prince repeated, gazing into Rusalka's eyes. "I would rather live beneath the waves with you than in my castle all alone."

With these words, Jezibaba appeared.

"If you join Rusalka beneath the surface of this lake, you can never again return to your castle or to the world of men," she said. "The decision you make will be final."

The prince stood firm. He never wanted to be parted from his Rusalka again. And so, he and the water nymph, still hand in hand, descended together into their watery kingdom.

THE
KING
and the
CHARCOAL
BURNER

It happened one day many centuries ago that the king of Bohemia, while riding in the forest with a hunting party, was separated from the others and lost.

In those days, the Bohemian forest was deep, dark, and home only to wild animals. And even those seemed scarce to the hungry king, whose meager diet of nuts, berries, and water left him more and more exhausted. Finally, on the seventh day, he heard merry folk music and the cheers and cries of celebration. He followed the sounds to the edge of a clearing, where he saw a humble hut, radiating festivity.

Happy beyond belief, the king stumbled toward the cottage. Nobody in the crowd recognized him as their king, for he was covered in mud, and the thorns and brambles of the forest had torn his royal clothing. Desperately he begged for food and shelter.

One woman rushed to help him off the ground. She was Anna, a charcoal burner's wife, and the mistress of the cottage. "You poor man, come in and join us. Rest your tired body and have some dinner. We are celebrating the Feast of St. Vaclav."

The king ate ravenously, and after some time the food and the merry atmosphere revived his spirits. Lidushka, the charcoal burner's beautiful daughter, came to his table and asked him if he would like to dance.

"I would be delighted," he answered with a smile. Together they whirled around the cabin, dancing and laughing happily. To Lidushka it seemed as though they were floating on a pillow of air. Never had she danced with so graceful a partner.

After their dance the tired revellers went outside to get a breath of fresh air, and Lidushka found herself confiding in the gentle stranger.

"My parents will not allow me to marry Jenik, who asked for my hand last spring. We love each other very much, but they hope to find a wealthy merchant for me. It has made me very sad. Thank you for lifting my spirits."

Meanwhile Jenik had been looking everywhere for Lidushka. When he stepped outside and saw her speaking with the stranger he became jealous. "Who do you think you are?" he shouted angrily. "Lidushka is not interested in you!"

Just as the king was about to respond, he glimpsed his men, some distance away, in the corner of his eye. He turned back to Lidushka. "I promise that some day, when it is in my power to do so, I shall help you as your family helped me," he said.

And with that he slipped away to join his entourage.

Some months later Bohemia was drawn into war with a neighboring kingdom, and Jenik joined the Bohemian army to defend his homeland. During a terrible battle Jenik saw that the king had been knocked from his horse. Jenik just managed to drag the barely conscious, armor-clad king to the edge of the battlefield. There he was met by the king's knights.

"You have acted most nobly in saving our master's life," they praised him. "You will be handsomely rewarded for your bravery and courage."

Jenik hardly paused to accept the men's congratulations before rushing off to rejoin his regiment in driving away the now-retreating invaders. Soon the battle was won.

From all over the Bohemian lands important people gathered to celebrate their victory. Lidushka, anxiously waiting to hear word from Jenik, was shocked to receive instead an invitation to the palace.

"What could the king possibly want with us?" she worried. When members of the castle guard arrived to accompany her and her parents, Lidushka became still more frightened.

The king and queen had assembled everyone in the central hall to thank the humble soldier who had saved the nation's sovereign in battle. As the ceremony began, the charcoal burner and his family were astounded to see that the guest of honor was none other than Jenik, clothed for the occasion in splendid new robes.

Jenik did not notice his friends in the crowd, so intent was he on not stumbling in his finery. As he walked toward the royal couple, he raised his eyes, and understanding slowly dawned. The man to whom he had acted so rudely in the charcoal burner's cottage was the king!

Jenik fell to his knees. "Your Highness, please forgive me! I had no idea that it was you with whom my beloved Lidushka was dancing."

"Young man, it is I who should be kneeling before you," said the king. "Twice now my life has been saved: once by your beloved Lidushka's family, who gave me shelter and food when I needed it, and the second time by you, who so courageously saved me from certain death in battle. Therefore, arise a knight, and stand by my side as a member of my court."

The king then called the charcoal burner and his family forward. Gravely, he placed Lidushka's hand in Jenik's. Then he turned to Lidushka's parents.

"I would be honored if you would permit me to arrange for the wedding of Lidushka and Jenik."

Joyously, the couple embraced, and Lidushka's parents blessed the king for everything he had done for them. And they all lived happily ever after.

KATE
AND THE
DEVIL

Long ago in Bohemia, the heart of Europe, it was customary in the autumn for every village to celebrate their bountiful crops. In one particular village, a great feast was underway at the local tavern; music was playing, and people young and old were singing and dancing.

One girl, however, sat alone in the corner, sullenly watching the festivities. Kate was a sulky, brooding girl, who rarely had a kind word for anybody. That evening not a single young man had asked her to dance.

Well, that was not exactly true. Jirka, the local shepherd, had noticed Kate's distress and asked her to dance with him, but Kate had refused. She was far too good for a humble shepherd! So Kate sat out dance after dance, waiting for a better partner: Honza, the church organ player; Mirek, the town's richest merchant; or even Karel, the most graceful dancer. But each of these young men was too tired, too hungry, or had promised the next dance to another.

Finally Kate lost patience. "If no one wants to dance with me, then to the devil with you all!" she shouted above the din. Forgetting all about Jirka's offer, she muttered crossly, "I'd partner the devil himself just to get out on the dance floor."

No sooner had she uttered these words than the tavern door flew open, and a handsome hunter strode straight up to Kate.

"I've traveled far to dance with you, Kate," he said, "all the way from my lands in the south. My name is Marbuel."

Kate was overjoyed that so elegant a man was showing an interest in her, and together they danced away the evening. He charmed her with tales about his estate, his riches, and the number of people who worked for him.

At last, someone worthy of me! thought Kate, smiling coyly and fluttering her lashes. "How I long to see where you live," she simpered.

Marbuel smiled at her. "Perhaps that can be arranged, dear Kate."

Kate and the Devil

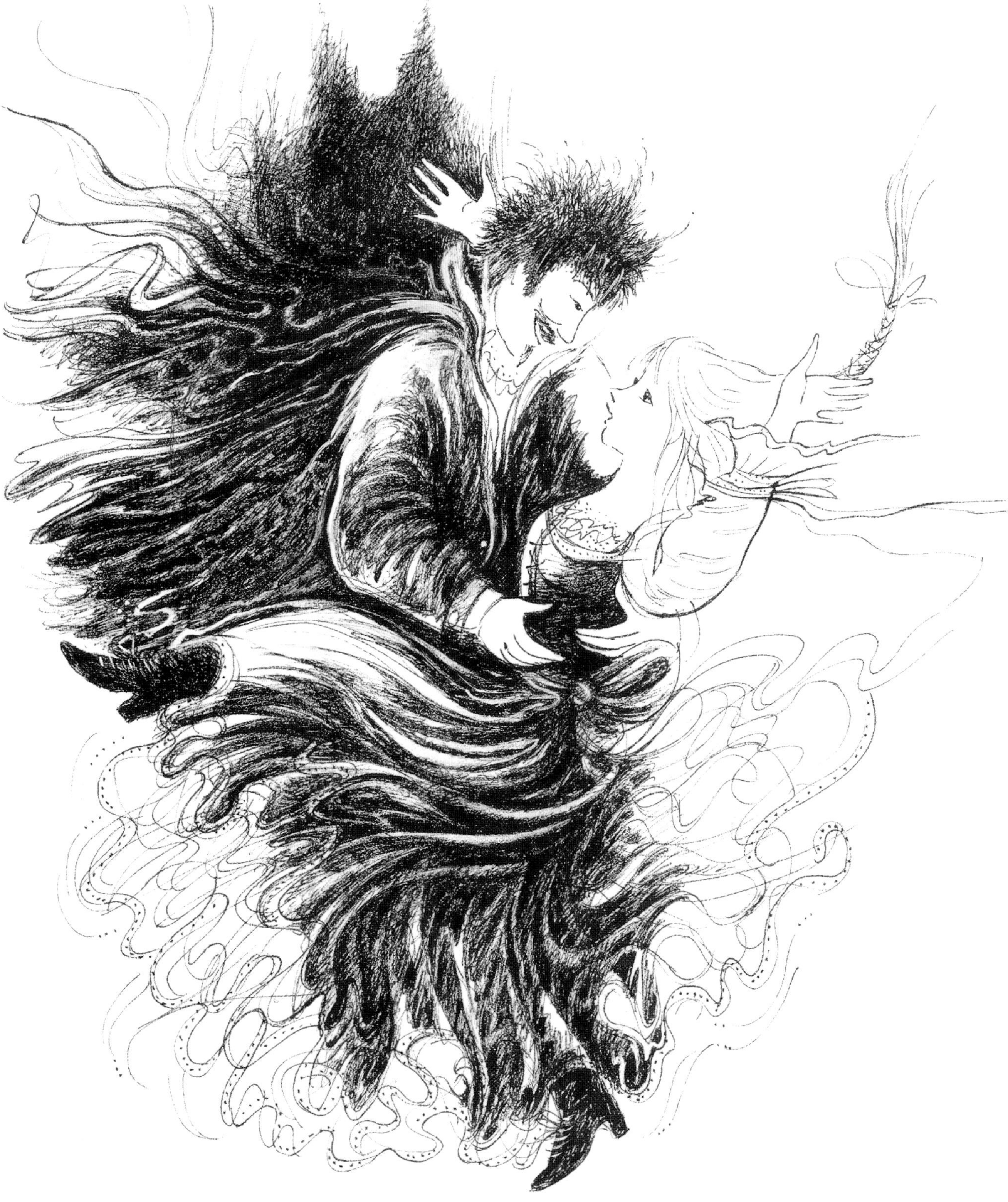

When the clock struck midnight, the lamps started to flicker strangely, and a deep, thunderous rumbling rose, drowning out the music. The dancers stopped mid-step, for the ground seemed to be trembling beneath their feet. Before their shocked eyes, the floor split in two, revealing a gaping abyss.

Marbuel grabbed Kate around the waist. "You shall visit my lands sooner than you thought!" he roared, and with these words, he leapt into the depths, dragging Kate along with him.

The terrified dancers were all frozen in place—all except Jirka, that is. He'd been suspicious of the stranger from the start. He dove into the pit after Kate, just as it was closing.

Deep beneath the earth, Lucifer, the king of Hell, awaited his servant Marbuel, who had been charged with investigating how the Bohemian queen was treating her subjects. At last Marbuel appeared at the gates, with a peasant girl riding on his back.

"You're jostling me! Slow down! Peeuw! Your country smells like rotten eggs, and it's far too hot. Hurry up, I want to see your mansion!" she nagged from his shoulders.

"This cannot be the queen whom you were ordered to bring before me! Marbuel, you idiot, who is this woman?" demanded Lucifer.

Marbuel quaked with fear. He regretted, now, the momentary lust for earthly pleasures that had pulled him away from his mission and into Kate's arms. "M-m-master, this is…Kate. She called me to dance, and now she won't leave me alone!"

"Well, get rid of her!" Lucifer roared. Kate jumped down from Marbuel's shoulders. "Who are you?" she demanded of Lucifer. "Marbuel, is this your servant? Well, he's awfully rude. And where are the riches you bragged about?"

Jirka, who had been hiding up to now, stepped forward. "Sir, perhaps I can be of some assistance. Open Hell's coffers and let Kate take what she wants. That will keep her quiet. Then, I will be more than happy to lead Marbuel straight to the queen whom you seek."

Meanwhile, the queen of Bohemia was having a leisurely breakfast in her castle. As she sipped her tea, three people appeared in a poof of sulphur.

"Your Majesty," said Jirka, "you have been consigned to Hell for your harsh treatment of your serfs. This devil has come to take you away." Jirka stepped closer to the queen and bowed low. Quietly, he added, "But if you promise to free your serfs, I will help you escape Lucifer's clutches."

The queen's face was the color of ashes, and she trembled with terror at the thought of spending eternity in the fiery depths of Hell.

"I swear to you on my royal throne that if you help me, all the serfs in Bohemia will be free," she choked.

Jirka turned around to face Kate, who was busy admiring the diamond rings and golden bracelets she had brought with her from Hell.

"Kate, where is that beautiful emerald tiara? You didn't leave it behind, did you?" he said in mock dismay.

"Oh my! Wouldn't that tiara look beautiful in my hair, Marbuel? We simply must go back and get it!"

Marbuel was horrified. "I would rather suffer at the hands of Lucifer for eternity than spend one more minute with Kate!" he cried. And with that, he vanished in a cloud of sulphurous smoke, never to be seen again.

The happy queen kept her promise, and freed every enslaved peasant in her kingdom. Clever Jirka became the queen's advisor and was given a beautiful estate where he and Kate lived happily dancing the nights away.

O moon, up in the deep sky,

your light shines far and wide;

you wander throughout the wide world

looking into people's homes.

O moon, stay a while,

tell me—where is my beloved!

Tell him, silver moon

that my arms embrace him,

so he might, at least for a moment

remember me in his arms.

Illuminate his way,

tell him who waits for him here!

Should a human soul dream of me,

may it wake him from that dream.

O moon, do not fade away!

Antonin Dvorak w
the Czechs and a s
much of what's best

Although he would eventually become one of Europe's greatest composers, Antonin Dvorak had comparatively humble origins. His father, Frantisek, was a butcher and tavern keeper in Nelahozeves, north of Prague, while his mother Anna (nee Zdenkova) was from a family of farmers. From an early age Antonin, or Tonik as his family called him, exhibited musical talent, regularly entertaining customers at the tavern with his fiddle playing. His first musical training was with the village schoolmaster, Josef Spitz (who doubled as the church organist). After six years of school Tonik apprenticed to his father in the butcher's trade for a year, a somewhat unhappy period for him: he was already deeply interested in music, but his

ANTONIN DVORAK (1841-1904)

father was convinced that his son should continue the family business.

Tonik was sent to nearby Zlonice the following year, where he stayed with his mother's bachelor brother, steward to Count Kinsky, in order to better learn his trade and improve his German, the official language of the Austro-Hungarian Empire. Here he had the good fortune to fall under the influence of Antonin Liehmann, the local school's German master and an accomplished amateur musician who gave Tonik lessons in viola, piano and organ. Tonik played in Liehmann's chamber music group, which performed regularly at the count's castle. Together they wrote the "Forget-Me-Not Polka," Antonin's first-ever composition.

Unfortunately, the future composer also had to devote time to his trade studies and endure lessons in German, activities that interested him a great deal less than music.

Tonik's second year at Zlonice was not as enjoyable as the first. His father had begun to suspect that Tonik was not devoting enough time to his apprenticeship, and as his business was faring poorly in Nelahozeves, he picked up the Dvorak family and moved to Zlonice. Under his father's watchful eye, Tonik's musical activity was severely restricted. However, Tonik's uncle saw how his nephew's talent was blossoming under Liehmann's encouragement and guidance. He pledged his financial support, and he and Liehmann convinced Tonik's father that it would be a crime for the young prodigy to pursue a career in anything other than music. They planned to send him to the Prague Organ School, where all classes were conducted in German; with such motivation, Tonik was content to spend some time polishing up his command of the language at a secondary school in Ceske Kamenice, a town near the border with Saxony whose inhabitants were all German-speaking.

The subsequent year Tonik and his father made the 26-mile journey on foot from Zlonice to Bohemia's capital city, Prague, pulling a cart of Tonik's belongings. He was to lodge in the Old Town with his cousin, Marie Plivova. However, her apartment was already rather crowded with her four young daughters, so Tonik was forced to move in with an uncle, Vaclav Dusek, a poor railway employee who lived on Charles Square. Upon finishing his studies at the organ school in July of 1859, Antonin Dvorak decided to stay in Prague, the musical heart of Bohemia. He made some money playing viola with a local band three nights a week, performing in the restaurants and inns of Prague. By a stroke of luck this group

ANTONIN DVORAK BIRTHPLACE IN NELAHOZEVES.

VIEW OF NELAHOZEVES VILLAGE NEAR PRAGUE.

became the nucleus of the orchestra for the newly opened Prozatimni Divadlo (Provisional Theatre) built specifically to stage performances of Czech opera and theatre. Dvorak played with this orchestra until 1871, when he quit in order to concentrate on composing. On the advice of Bedrich Smetana, who had conducted the Provisional Theatre orchestra since 1866, Dvorak wrote *The King and the Charcoal Burner*. His first attempt was a disaster. Performers found it impossible to stage, and Dvorak was obliged to withdraw it while it was still in rehearsal. He would later rewrite this opera, which was finally performed in 1874.

Most of the 1870s were years of poverty for Dvorak; to make ends meet he took on a position as organist at St. Adalbert's Church in the New Town, as well as numerous students. He fell in love with one of them, Josefina, who rejected him in favor of Count Kounic of Vysoka; in 1873, he married Josefina's sister, Anna. For the next four years the couple struggled, living almost entirely off the Austrian State Stipendium which Dvorak won three times between 1874 and 1877. His last entry, "Moravian Duets", captivated one of the judges, Johannes Brahms, who recommended their "piquant charm" to his own publisher, Fritz Simrock. Up to that point, Dvorak had only a single work in print. Now, "Slavonic Dances" and "Moravian Duets," both published by Simrock, got rave reviews, propelling Dvorak to stardom in Europe and the United States.

With the money from these successes,

Dvorak purchased some land from his brother-in-law the count, 40 miles southwest of Prague, and built a single-story house on the foundations of a shepherd's cottage there. Here he spent most of his summers, raising pigeons and sitting by the pond that became the inspiration for *Rusalka*. He also loved to walk in solitude early in the morning through the forests surrounding his house.

By 1879 Dvorak's published works had made their way to England, where they garnered glowing reviews. In 1884 he made his first trip to London, where he conducted in the Royal Albert Hall and was made an honorary member of the Philharmonic Society of London. Of one of his trips to London he wrote to a friend: "Everywhere I appear, whether in the street or at home or even when I go into a shop to buy something, people crowd around me ask for my autograph. There are pictures of me at all the booksellers and people buy them only to have some memento."

By his third visit to London in 1885 Dvorak's music was being heard as far from his home as Melbourne, Australia.

In 1891 Dvorak was appointed Professor of Composition at the Prague Conservatory, a position interrupted by a telegram from Vienna inviting him to be Director of the New Conservatory of Music in New York. After much deliberation he accepted, and left the following year with his wife, eldest daughter, Otylia and son, Antonin. Stepping out from his apartment on East 17th Street, Dvorak wandered around the city with a little notebook always in hand, picking out melodies he heard folk musicians play in local taverns, frequently incorporating them as motifs in his compositions.

During his three years in America Dvorak dearly missed his beloved Bohemia. But there were many things in the New World to distract him. He had always been an avid trainspotter—legend has it that back in Prague, he occasionally sent a student down to Franz Josef Station to catch the number of an elusive steam engine! In New York's Grand Central Station only passengers were allowed on the platforms. So, Dvorak would travel by elevated train to 155th street where he could watch the Chicago and Boston express trains go by. The harbor was much nearer, and Dvorak soon cultivated an interest in large ocean liners, which were a rather uncommon sight in land-locked Bohemia. He delighted in inspecting ships, taking every opportunity to speak with their captains and crews, and soon knew them all by name. The composer also found comfort in feeding pigeons in Central Park.

His homesickness was eased in 1893 by a summer stay in the Czech-speaking community of Spillville, Iowa, where he was joined by the four children he had left behind in Bohemia. It was here that he put the finishing touches on what would come to be known as the *New World* Symphony, which was performed that December to an ecstatic public at Carnegie Hall. On his way back to New York from Iowa he stopped at Niagara Falls with his family. "My goodness!" exclaimed the awe-struck composer. "That will be a symphony in B Minor!"

He returned to Bohemia in 1895 where he resumed his duties at the Prague Conservatory, becoming director in 1901. Three years later, on May 1st, he died. He was 63.

IAN AND VLADYANA KRYKORKA IN FRONT OF THE NATIONAL THEATRE
IN PRAGUE, WHERE RUSALKA PREMIERED ON MARCH 31, 1901